You are an Amazing Girl

A Collection of Inspiring Stories about Courage, Friendship, Inner Strength and Self-Confidence

Nadia Ross

Special Art Stories

You are an Amazing Girl

A Collection of Inspiring Stories about Courage, Friendship, Inner Strength and Self-Confidence

Nadia Ross

HARDCOVER ISBN: 9791255530763

support@specialartbooks.com
www.specialartbooks.com

Table of Contents

Introduction

Hello! Do you know that you are a wonderful girl?

You are very special. You are the only you there is in the entire world, and that's out of billions of people! You are smart, funny, courageous, and unique, which is something you should always remember. You bring an amazing light into this world that no one else can bring, and only you know how you can shine.

There are many challenges the world will offer you. Sometimes they are big, and sometimes they are smaller. These challenges may make you afraid, or you may feel doubt about what you are doing. But just so you know, we all feel these feelings! Your parents, grandparents, friends, siblings, and even people you don't know

doubt their choices and actions sometimes. They also get scared too.

I want to let you in on a little secret, though. Even when things scare you, you can still do them! Sometimes, the things you fear the most are the ones that give you the best experience! You can learn from mistakes and find goodness in everything you do, even when it doesn't feel so good.

This book will introduce you to a group of girls who go through the same things you do every day. They are scared, worried, and sometimes, they don't win right away. They work hard, learn from mistakes, and keep trying. These girls get discouraged, doubt their abilities, and sometimes they almost give up, but somewhere deep inside of them, their light shines through. They find their courage and self-confidence and push through their difficult moments to reach their ultimate goals.

You can shine your light in your corner of the world, and you can bring that light to other people when you let go of fear and keep learning lessons. When you believe in yourself, you can accomplish anything. You are a wonderful girl.

Luna the Curious

How curious are you to try new things? Do you see things that make you feel excited? Are you eager to try new things? Do you keep going until you find something that "fits" for you? You don't have to be anxious about deciding what to do with life. You don't have to make a choice right away, either. You can take your time to find your passion. What you do with your life is your own, and when you decide with your heart, you can't go wrong!

~ ~ ~

Luna was curious about everything. She loved learning about new things so much that many of her family members called her "Luna the Curious." Luna didn't mind, though, and she was proud to try everything that came her way and thrilled to look for new things. She had tried many things in her life and always put her heart and soul into it. Some of her favorite things she found to do so far were playing the trumpet, running around in the woods, splashing in the water, reading books, playing in her front yard, drawing, painting, talking on her mom's cell phone to her grandma, baking muffins, playing card games, swimming, riding her bicycle, and many other things.

But one thing that other people had that she didn't have, was something special that was her *thing*. Luna's mom was a painter, her dad was a baker, her sister was a basketball player, and her brother enjoyed writing. While she knew they liked to do other things, they each focused on their one *thing*.

So, Luna decided that she would start searching for one thing too.

She looked at everything she had tried and thought about what she liked the most. Out of all the things she had already done, roller-skating, playing music, and reading books were her favorite. But she wasn't sure if reading books was her *thing*. She liked to be busy and moving, and she only read stories right before bedtime or when her teacher gave her reading homework. So, she crossed it off of her list. That left playing music and roller-skating as two *things* she wanted to try.

Although she didn't know what she could do with roller-skating, she knew she had to try it out. She went to her parents and asked them if she could try roller-skating lessons and learn how to play the trumpet for real. Her parents looked at each other and smiled. It was a smile that told Luna that she was true to herself and that they were happy to help her find her *thing*. This smile made Luna so pleased.

Within the next few weeks, Luna focused only on roller-skating and playing the trumpet. They were both fun to do, but it wasn't what Luna wanted to do as a full-time *thing*. She did finish out her trumpet lessons and the six-week skating session, but explained to her mom and dad that she didn't want to keep going any longer.

Next, Luna asked her sister to teach her about basketball. She thought that maybe the love of the game would run in the family, and while basketball was fun, she didn't feel in her heart that the game was her *thing*. Luna also asked her brother about writing, but she wasn't a fan of writing either. Luna was starting to worry she may never find her *thing*.

At dinner one night, Luna sighed loudly. Her dad looked at her mom and raised his eyebrow as they silently wondered what was wrong with Luna. Her mom shrugged her shoulders, and so her dad nodded. "Luna, what is wrong?"

Luna shrugged her shoulders, and she always felt comfortable talking with her family because they supported her through everything, so she said, "I'm not sure I'll ever find my *thing*. You're a baker, Mom is a painter, Sofie likes basketball, and Braden likes to write. I like to do a lot of things, but I don't have one thing I like to do the most. Everything I've tried doesn't feel quite like *IT*."

Her mom smiled at her. "Luna, you are still very young. You have a lot of time to find one thing. And even when you do, you might want to change it up after a while. Dad wasn't always a baker; he used to work in an office and draw build-ings. I didn't always paint for my job ei-ther; I used to work in a bank."

Luna thought for a moment. "What made you want to work at a bank?"

Her mom shook her head. "I didn't really. It was just a job to help pay bills while I looked for my real *thing*. It took me a while to figure out too. Trust me, if you keep looking, you are going to find something you love most of all."

Luna nodded. Her mom's advice and her family's support made her feel better. It helped her to know that they were rooting for her. Even if it was taking her longer than she thought it would.

"Tell you what," her dad said. "You like baking with me. Why don't you come to the bakery tomorrow, and I'll show you something new."

Luna's interest perked up, and she couldn't contain her curiosity. She got so excited and said, "What is new?"

"Ah-ha, sweetie. You will have to wait until tomorrow."

Luna nodded as her curiosity made her bounce the whole time she helped clear the table.

The next morning, Luna and her dad woke up when it was still very dark outside. *Working at a bakery is early, early morning work,* Luna thought sleepily. It was one reason she knew that being a baker was not her *thing*, but she liked going with her dad once in a while.

Luna's dad invited her to stand behind the metal table with many silver gadgets when they got there. "We are making muffins today. Here," he said as he handed her metal measuring cups. "You have to measure out 380 grams of flour. It has to be exact. It cannot be over or under, otherwise our muffins won't work."

She took a shaky breath. Her dad always said that it was very precise work and her hands weren't old enough yet. Luna guessed they were old enough now. She nodded and shook herself awake a little more.

This time was important. This job was important. She needed to be awake and aware.

Luna scooped out the flour with a measuring cup and scraped off the top to be completely level. Then she weighed the flour on the scale. She found that every time she leveled off flour, it was very satisfying.

It was so satisfying that it *almost* felt like her *thing*. She definitely wanted to do it more, but it didn't feel quite right.

The next day she went to school, they introduced a new subject called Science. In science, the teacher described, there can be a lot of measuring and mixtures to do experiments and help figure things out. The teacher also said that curiosity is an important part of science because you can discover new things and find new ways to help people when your experiments pay off. Luna quickly thought about how measuring out the flour yesterday felt really good. She also knew that she was a *very* curious person!

She raised her hand to ask her teacher, "When will we be doing science experiments?"

The teachers smiled. "Not for a few weeks, but after we have a science fair where you will be able to create an experiment all yourself, bring it in for the school to see, and maybe even win a ribbon."

While the thought of a ribbon was exciting, Luna couldn't wait to get home to ask her family about doing science experiments. She hadn't ever felt something like this before, and for some reason, Luna knew that for now, science was going to be her thing!

~ ~ ~

Just like Luna, never give up looking for your *thing*. You are a special girl who is one of a kind. Only you can think as you do. Only you can do what you are going to do! Take time to find what you love to do, and decide with your heart. Be true to yourself, and it will be amazing.

Nicole in a New School

Going to school can be fun and exciting. You get to learn new things and you get an opportunity to meet new people.

When you have to do something new that you've never done before, do you feel nervous? Maybe you can be afraid that new people you meet won't like you or think you can't make new friends. Sometimes when we try something new, our nerves kick in and we think that the fear we feel has to do with something bad, when really it just means we haven't done it before.

You are unique, smart, and very special. Having fears and nerves when something new is coming up is normal. Finding a way to let out your nerves with your creativity can help you see that when something is new, it doesn't mean it's bad. It just means that it is unknown, and once you see that your nerves won't stop you, you can show everyone how amazing you truly are.

~ ~ ~

This morning, Nicole lay awake in her bedroom. She stared at the ceiling fan and watched it spin. This ceiling fan wasn't the fan that she used to look up at. That one was white with little pink flowers. This fan was a new one, in a new room, in a new house, in a new town far away from her old one.

She was still getting used to the idea that they had moved from one place to another, and now she would have to go to a new school where she didn't know anyone. Nicole began to feel butterflies in her belly late last night because she was so nervous. Now, she could see shadows from the sun start to rise against her ceiling. She didn't know what time it was, but she definitely hadn't slept very much.

This year, everything would be new. She would have new people in her class, and she would have a new teacher. She was very nervous.

Nicole was worried about making friends. Would anyone talk to her? Each class had to sit together for lunch. Who would she eat lunch with? What did they play during recess? Would anyone ask her to run around with them, or would she just sit on a swing by herself?

That thought made her very sad and made her miss her old friends.

Then, a thought hit her like lightning, and she sat up quickly. To get to know new people, Nicole would make friendship bracelets for everyone in her class. This idea made her jump out of bed and she started planning out how she would do this. If everyone in her class had a friendship bracelet, they would have a new way to connect. That was the way she was going to make new friends! Her idea made the butterflies in her belly go away, and she became excited for the first day of school.

In class, she couldn't stop smiling, and it turned out that the two students who sat next to her were very friendly. And although she was excited about making the friendship bracelets, she kept the idea a secret from them because she wanted the bracelets to be a surprise.

At recess, Nicole wasn't worried about being herself around new people any longer. She ran up to the students who sat next to her in class, and they asked her to play with them right away. She gladly accepted.

When she went home, she ran into the kitchen to tell her mom about her first school day, and she asked her mom for some help. "There are twenty five children in my class and I will need supplies of thread to make them all bracelets," she said.

Her mom smiled and said, "After dinner then, we will go to the craft store."

Nicole couldn't wait to start on her bracelets, but first, she had to do homework and then she wanted to reach out to her friends from her old school and see how their first day back at school went.

When she got in touch with them, the girls all exchanged their first day of school stories. Nicole became a little sad because she missed her friends, but when she told her friends about making the friendship bracelets, they thought it was a great idea and they decided to make bracelets for everyone in their class too.

"It will be like we are all united!" Nicole said.

Each day after school and her homework was done, Nicole and her friends went onto their video chat, made bracelets, and talked to one another for a little while. Nicole thought it was nice to speak to her friends every day and realized that not everything had to change just because she was across the country. They wouldn't be able to hang out like they used to, but if they continued to talk to one another through video chat, they could still keep in touch.

While Nicole was making her bracelets, she also thought about all the new friends she made at school. She thought about how none of the children in her class were the same, and decided to make different bracelets for each person.

Before the day she was going to take the bracelets to school, she got a package in the mail. When her mom gave the package to her, she looked up at her mom, confused. "What is this?" she asked.

Her mom said, "I don't know, sweetie. I think you'll have to open it to find out." Nicole noticed a little smirk on her mom's face and didn't understand what it meant, but Nicole knew that it meant something.

Nicole then turned her attention to the small package in her hands. Eagerly, she unwrapped the brown paper around the package and took out a small white box. On the top of the box, there was a card, and when Nicole opened it she saw that it was from her two friends who lived in her old town. Nicole looked up to her mother in shock. "They sent me a present?" She took the lid off and found a friendship bracelet of her very own.

"Oh my goodness!" Nicole cheered. "I can't believe they sent one of these over to me." She started tearing up with joy. Her mom took the bracelet from her hand and started to tie it around her wrist.

"Yes," her mom said. "You make very good friends. They called me for the address last week. I had to keep it a secret from you."

"Oh, wow," Nicole exclaimed. She looked at the bracelet in amazement. "I can't believe they did that."

"They wanted you to have a bracelet too. That way, everyone in your class will be united." Her mom smiled and hugged Nicole. "Now, it's time for bed."

Nicole went to bed but couldn't fall asleep. She continually looked at her bracelet or felt for it. She really did have amazing friends. She was very touched and thrilled that she would be able to share in the fun of getting a new bracelet. She was hoping all her classmates would feel the way she had when she got her bracelet too.

The next day, Nicole was finally ready to give the bracelets to all the kids in her class. Even though she had started making friends with a lot of other kids in her class, she still kept her presents a secret. She brought in her box of twenty five bracelets and started to feel the butterfly wings flapping again in her tummy. This time, though, Nicole realized that the butterflies were there because she was excited.

After Nicole passed out all the bracelets, she helped her new friends put them on and added the last bracelet to her wrist, saying, "Now we are all united!" She raised her arm into the air to show off her bracelet and was so pleased when all the other students raised their arms as well.

Nicole realized that being creative was the best way she could have gotten over her nerves. And because of her idea, she got to make a lot of new friends.

~ ~ ~

Do you know that you are creative even when you are feeling nervous? Do you think your creativity is a way to help connect people and get rid of any nervous or scared feelings? When you look positively at your emotions, even if they make you feel a little weird, you can do amazing things. The special and wonderful way you look at the world will help you connect with people in fantastic ways! Now, show the world how amazing you are.

Sara's Big Assignment

Have you ever been afraid of doing something and worried that you wouldn't do very well? Some school projects can take hours or even days! Do you try your hardest to get the best results you possibly can? How much time would you put into it? How nervous would you get when you turn the project in? Don't worry, wonderful girl, your nerves just mean you care, and when you work hard, you learn amazing lessons. When you learn those lessons, you have a great time.

~ ~ ~

Sara came home one day in a panic. She rushed into the house, threw down her book bag, and ran to her mother. "Mom! I have a huge project due at the end of the week. It's going to take me so long. I cannot believe my teacher did this to us!"

Sara's mom smiled. She knew that Sara was always nervous about new projects because she liked to do well in school. "Your teacher wouldn't have given that project to you if she didn't think you could do it. What do you have to do?"

"I have to create a solar system with all the planets and their moons. It has to be a 3D model, and I have to turn it in on Friday. I have to build it!" Sara was really nervous because she had never built anything for school. The most she had ever built was a few blocks on top of each other.

"Do you have the homework assignment with the rules for the project?"

"Yes!" Sara said. She ran down the hallway to get her book bag and ran back into the kitchen. Her mom raised an eyebrow at her and held up her hand.

"Sara," her mom said. "You need to calm down and take a deep breath. And stop running in the house, you know that is against the rules."

Sara listened to her mom. She did close her eyes when she took a deep breath. Sara realized that her mom was right. The teacher wouldn't have given the project to the class if they weren't ready for it. But the project was so big, she knew she would have to start it right away.

"Mom, we are going to need a bunch of supplies," Sara said.

Sara's mom smiled. She knew Sara was ready to tackle the project. "Okay, but you are missing the first steps, so why don't you plan out what kind of model you'd like to make and we will start from there."

Sara nodded. She reviewed the different ways to make a 3D solar system and realized many ways to do it. In the end, she decided that she would want to do a solar system display inside a box so it would be easy to carry.

And although her mom didn't tell her to do it, Sara started making a list of tools, items, and planets she would need.

Sara decided that she would need to get styrofoam balls of different sizes for the moons too. She would need paint, colored paper, skewers, glue, and a few other items.

After Sara finished her other homework and ate dinner with her family, her dad and mom went with Sara and her list to the store. As Sara walked around the store, she checked off each item she put into the basket. It was really hard for Sara not to put more in the basket than she had on her list. There were so many awesome things at the craft store. Sara wanted to touch them all. But she kept reminding herself that she needed to stay focused. She needed to start on her project that night because the solar system was big! And if she didn't start the project now, she might not get it done.

When the basket was full of items, they took the things to the check-out so her parents could pay for the supplies, and then they left.

After they got home, Sara set out all the items she needed to paint. There was a lot of stuff. Sara started to feel overwhelmed. She didn't know if she would be able to paint all of the planets, moons, and stars she planned on doing. Sara was worried she wouldn't get any-thing done in time, and if she did get something done, she was nervous that it wouldn't be her best work. She really didn't know where to start.

Sara remembered what her mom said about relaxing, closing her eyes, and taking a deep breath. So she did.

When she blew her breath out, she realized that she would just start with one styrofoam ball and then move on to the next. She wrote out a plan and realized that it wasn't as much work as it seemed it would be. If she painted tonight and tomorrow, she would have two days to put things together after.

Now that she had a plan, Sara worked very hard for the rest of the week. There were still times that she got a little nervous about the project, but when she would she would breathe and tell herself that everything was going to be okay.

Sara looked at her solar system assignment when the project came due and worried that it wouldn't be good enough. Her mom helped her carry the project into the school, and when Sara saw the other student's projects, she recognized that she had done a good job. She added all the planets, their moons, some stars, and the sun. Her project looked as good as many of the other kids', and she saw that her nerves were not needed.

When Sara and her mom set her solar system down, Sara realized that she was proud of herself for getting the work done and that the project looked very nice. She remembered how worried she was at the beginning of the week and saw the outcome of her hard work and planning. Sara now knew that even when her nerves got the better of her, if she closed her eyes, took a deep breath, and planned some things out, everything would be great because she was a smart and determined girl.

~ ~ ~

Well, what do you think? Do you know that no matter what happens, you will be able to do something difficult? Even when you think you won't be able to, you need to try it and do it anyway because, with a little practice and a little help, you can definitely achieve your goals! Remember to close your eyes, take a deep breath, and know that you can do anything you set your mind to.

Find Your Footing

When you are courageous, brave, and strong, you can overcome your fears. Even the biggest challenges can come with scary moments, and it's how you deal with them that matters most! Think

about what would happen to you when you fall? How would you get back up despite difficult situations? Keep going after your passion, of course!

~ ~ ~

Mila was dizzy with excitement. Today she was getting her cast off of her leg! Not only would she no longer have to walk with a cast, but she could also start skateboarding again. She couldn't wait to feel the board under her feet and the wind in her hair as she skated down her driveway.

Mila actually hurt herself when she tried a new trick, but she knew that sometimes people hurt themselves. And that when you do something you love, you will still face a few bumps and bruises.

As she got the cast removed, her mom asked the doctor, "How long until she can skateboard again? She has been itching to get back out there." Her mom placed her hand on Mila's shoulder, which made Mila smile. She took a deep breath. Knowing that her mom was always there was comforting. But her mom was right, Mila had been itching to get out on it and worked to make her skateboard better the entire six weeks her cast was on. She had put on new wheels, oiled them, tightened the bolts and more! Every day she had the skateboard in her hand in some way, daydreaming of when she would be able to get back to it.

Mila looked at the doctor expectantly, holding her breath for his answer. Finally, he said, "She should still wait a few days until she is more stable on her feet. And after that, she should only do small things at first." The doctor looked at Mila now. "You don't want to get hurt again, do you?"

Mila didn't know how to respond, she knew in her head that sometimes you get hurt, but when she asked her heart, her heart was scared by what the doctor had said.

Her mom took her hand and said, "Thank you, doctor; I'm sure she will be careful."

As Mila took a step, she thought she felt her leg wobble a little. Then she felt that the doctor might be right. Maybe she should wait a couple of days until she tried out her board.

At home, Mila realized she didn't even want to look at her skateboard. She was just too worried about her leg. Her head told her not to be scared that this was normal, but she couldn't shake that fear starting to balloon inside her chest.

After a few days, Mila kept finding ways to make herself busy. She decided to help do more chores, study for more tests, or even play more with her baby brother. Everything else seemed much more important than getting back on her skateboard.

The next week, Mila's mom sat down and asked Mila to sit with her. "I think we should talk," her mom said.

"Am I in trouble?" Mila asked. She thought that her mom only talked to her when something serious happened, like a low grade or fighting with her brother and sisters.

Her mom smiled, and Mila felt calmer. "No, I want to talk to you about why you are avoiding your skateboard."

Mila bit her lip. She didn't think it had been so clear to anyone else but her. She looked at her hands. "I don't know." Even though she did know what the problem was—she was afraid of getting hurt, and she didn't really want to talk about it because she was embarrassed by how she felt.

"Mila," her mom said, taking her hand. Mila looked at her mom. "I think you do know."

Mila blinked. Although she was having a hard time looking her mom in the eye, she said, "Yeah," in a very quiet voice.

"So, why do you think you aren't skating yet?"

Mila shook her head and felt tears starting to run over her cheeks. "I am afraid!" she said.

Her mom put an arm around her shoulder and said to her, "It's okay to be afraid, sweetie. But just because you are scared doesn't mean you should stop doing what you love to do."

Mila nodded. She knew her mom was right, and she also felt so much better after she admitted out loud that she was scared. That surprised her. She thought that maybe any time she was feeling bad, perhaps she should talk about it. It would make her feel better.

"Do you want to go try it now?" Mila's mom asked. "I can be there with you, and you only have to go on the flat part of the driveway."

Mila wiped her tears away from her cheeks and nodded. "Yes." She was still afraid, but she knew her mom was right. She shouldn't stop skateboarding, be-cause she loved it.

The moment Mila grabbed her board and went outside, she started to feel like her old self. Her fear was still there, but the comfort her skateboard gave her pushed the fear away.

The sun was shining, and the breeze was slightly blowing. Mila took a step out of the shadow and placed her skateboard on the ground. She blew out a big breath and she realized a lot of her fear went with it.

"Would you like me to hold your hand?" her mom asked.

Mila shook her head no; she wanted to do this alone.

She put one foot on the skateboard and lined it up with her other foot. She closed her eyes and let another big breath out, and another part of her fear went with it. She pushed off with her foot that was on the ground, and away she went. A smile broke out across her face as all her happiness came rushing back.

She couldn't believe she let fear take away her happiness! But she was so glad that even though she was scared, she overcame it!

She felt good and whole again as she stopped her board, turned around, and beamed an even bigger smile at her mother. Mila picked her board up in one hand and ran to her mom. She threw herself into her mom's arms for a big hug!

Mila would never let fear stop her again.

~ ~ ~

Now that Mila has found out that fear won't stop her, do you think you will let fear stop you? If you love something, you have to keep at it to be happy and enjoy what you do! Don't let fear stop you from living your dreams! You are special! You deserve to do everything you want to do!

Lucy Bakes a Cake

Have you ever tried so hard to do something, but failed to get a good result? Maybe you got discouraged and wanted to quit. This is exactly what happened to the character of our next story. Lucy wanted to make a perfect cake, but more than a few things didn't go exactly as she expected.

What do you think happens? Let's keep reading to find out!

~ ~ ~

Lucy has tried a lot of cakes in her life, but chocolate cake is her favorite. If you ask Lucy, she'll tell you that she loves chocolate cake. Recently Lucy found out that she can make cakes with her own two hands. When her mom told her about cake recipes, Lucy found herself very excited and couldn't wait to start baking.

Since she hadn't baked a cake before, her mom found a recipe on the internet and Lucy was thrilled to try it out. But Lucy didn't want any other help from her mom—except for turning on the oven. Lucy was so excited, and she couldn't wait to try her cake. The first thing she did was get a bowl out. She poured all the ingredients into the bowl and mixed them. When she was done, her mom put the pan into the oven, and Lucy set the timer.

Her mom offered to help Lucy, but Lucy still refused. "I want to do this mostly on my own, Mom. It's very important to me."

Lucy's mom smiled, put a comforting hand on her shoulder, and went into the other room. Lucy stayed in the kitchen doing homework. After a while, Lucy began to smell something unusual. She looked up and saw that smoke was starting to come out of the oven, just as her mom came in and said, "Lucy, did you forget to turn on the timer? It smells like burnt cake in here."

Her mom looked at the oven and rushed to it. She opened the door, tried to wave the smoke away, and took the burnt cake outside to cool off. Lucy sat there and was shocked. She had set the time to see it, but she forgot to press the START button. Lucy put her head into her hands and shook it in disbelief.

"I forgot to hit the start button on the timer," Lucy wailed as her mom came back in.

"That's okay, Lucy," her mom said. "Next time you'll know to start the timer. Everyone makes mistakes, especially when they are trying something new. I'll still help you, if you want me to."

Lucy shook her head *No*, she did want to do this on her own, even though she was starting to feel a little nervous.

The next day, Lucy put all the ingredients into the bowl, mixed everything up, put the mixture into the cake pan, and her mom put it into the oven. Lucy made sure to set the time *and* hit the START button. *Nothing can go wrong now!* Lucy thought.

But Lucy was wrong. When the timer went off, Lucy ran to see how her cake looked— because it smelled great! But the center of the cake had fallen into itself. It looked like a crater on the moon.

"What happened now?" Lucy asked her mother.

"I don't know, sweetie. Sometimes cakes just don't bake right. Did you put the in- gredients in the way the directions said to?"

Lucy slapped her forehead. She didn't know there were directions! She only saw the ingredients list. Tomorrow she would try again! She really wanted to eat that cake.

The third cake that Lucy made, she read over the instructions and put every ingredient into the bowl that she was supposed to. When the cake came out of the oven, it wasn't burnt and it wasn't sunken in. Lucy was so excited she clapped her hands and couldn't wait until the cake cooled down.

After dinner, Lucy and her mom each had a slice of cake, but something just wasn't right . . . Lucy found something crunchy in her slice. She looked at her mom, who was also pulling out pieces of eggshells from her mouth. "What did I do wrong now?" Lucy said. She had been learning from all her mistakes, but she was starting to get frustrated. "Maybe I'm not cut out for baking," she said and put her head in her hands. "Maybe I should just leave it up to other people and just go back to eating cake."

"Lucy," her mom said. "That is no way to look at things. Each time you've made your cake, you've made a different mistake. This time you'll remember to look for eggshells. You are not the first person to accidentally burn a cake or have a cake cooked unevenly. You aren't the last person to forget to check for eggshells, either. You keep going, and I know you're going to bake an amazing cake."

Lucy nodded and felt a lot better. She trusted what her mom said and knew her mom was right. She hugged her and started to plan on baking another cake the next day.

After school the next day, Lucy came home and did her homework. She was a little less excited to rush into something like she had the first day and wanted to make sure she read the instructions and turned the timer on, plus she needed to check the mixture to see if any eggshells had accidentally fallen in.

Once again, her mom put the cake pan in the oven, and Lucy crossed her fingers and scrunched her eyes up, said a wish, and walked away from the baking cake. But not too far away because she was afraid that something else might happen to it if she went out of the room.

The cake smelled great, and it looked great too! Lucy found herself getting more excited. After the cake cooled off, she iced it with chocolate icing.

After dinner, Lucy and her mom had some chocolate cake. It was delicious! There were no crunchy eggs, and it was so chocolatey, fluffy, and good.

Lucy was very happy she listened to her mom and kept trying, even when she was worried that things wouldn't go right. She was excited to try more cake recipes and see what other yummy cakes she could make.

~ ~ ~

Remember! Don't be discouraged any time you try something and fail. There is no need to get down about it. Look at each opportunity as a new change to learn something new, like Lucy. Never give up, and you'll go so far!

Sofia Makes a New Friend

Do you like playing with your friends? Do you enjoy being around people who make you happy and who you can have fun with? Your friends think you are very special. You are kind, thoughtful, funny,

and brave. You think about others, and you help them out. But did you ever wonder what would happen if you had a bad day and your friends couldn't help you out? Did you ever think that making a new friend would help you see the world in a new way? Well, let's see how it helps Sofia. She has a lot of friends, but can they help her with a bad day? What if a new friend who sees the world differently can help her see things in another way.

~ ~ ~

Sofia enjoyed playing with her friends after school. Each day, when the weather was nice, she would go to the community playground with her mom and dad and meet a few of her friends so she could run around and get some energy out. Sofia and her friends always played pretend.

They played camping, cooking, going on an adventure, and many other creative things. Using her imagination was one of her favorite things to do, and her friends always liked the stories she came up with. One day, it started to rain when they were playing, and all the moms and dads and friends had to scatter back home.

Sofia was a little bummed because they didn't finish playing out their story, and now they probably wouldn't. As they were walking to the car, Sofia slipped on a wet patch of cement, and she fell on her knee, which left a scratch. It bled a little bit, and she cried because she didn't like to see her blood.

When she got home, her dad cleaned her up and put a Bandaid on it. She started to feel a little silly because of how much she cried, because the scrape really didn't hurt *that* much. After she was cleaned up, they went to have dinner. At the table, Sofia couldn't wait to eat, and instead of listening to her mom about the hot mashed potatoes, she stuck them in her mouth and burnt her tongue.

By the end of the night, she had bumped her head, scraped her elbow, dropped and broke a plate, she got a paper cut from reading her book, and she couldn't find the stuffed lion she usually slept with.

So many bad things happened to her at one time, she became very grumpy.

"Well..." her mom said, stroking Sofia's hair. "Hopefully, you will sleep it off and wake up feeling better."

But that didn't happen.

Sofia woke up even grumpier because, for some reason she was even more tired.

Even though her family tried to talk to her throughout breakfast, Sofia would barely mumble a response. On the bus, when her friend, Nya, sat down next to her and asked her how she was doing, Sofia grumbled that she was "fine" but that she "didn't feel like talking this morning." As she walked down the school hall, her friends waved to her and her teachers said good morning. But Sofia was having none of it.

They didn't know what a bad night she'd had, and she didn't want to talk about it with them. She was tired and sore, and her tongue still hurt from the too-hot mashed potatoes. Although she knew the bad mood wouldn't last forever, she just figured to let herself be grumpy because nothing seemed to be going her way.

When class started, Sofia realized she had forgotten to go to the bathroom and asked to use the hall pass. Although she could tell the teacher was a little annoyed, Sofia's teacher gave the nod and said, "Be back soon." Sofia nodded in response, and it wasn't like she forgot on purpose!

When she was walking down the hall, she noticed a boy using metal crutches to walk to the boy's bathroom. He had a grownup with him, and they went into the bathroom at the same time. Sofia thought *I would hate to go to the toilet with a grownup.* She had never seen that boy before, but her school was pretty big. She was sure she wouldn't see him again.

But she was wrong.

She saw him again at lunch, and while the grownup next to him helped carry his lunch tray, the boy sat down by himself. Sofia watched as the boy took the crutches off of his arms and watched him try to eat. He couldn't seem to open up his applesauce, and when he did, applesauce dripped all over him. He just laughed, shook his head, and wiped the spot off his shirt.

Then, she saw him drop a fork on the floor. Although the grownup with him picked up the fork and went to get him a new one, he didn't seem frustrated at all. The boy noticed Sofia watching him and waved to her.

Sofia, a bit embarrassed by getting caught but curious about the boy, could only wave back. After lunch was over, she went up to him and said, "Hello, are you new here?"

"Yeah, I started last week, but the teachers had to get me situated. My name is Tom."

"Hello, Tom. I'm Sofia. Do you want help carrying your bookbag?"

"Nope, I've got it," she watched as he shrugged the bookbag on in an awkward way, but he didn't seem bothered by it at all. "It makes me stronger," Tom said with a grin, where two of his teeth were missing.

Despite her grumpy mood, Sofia couldn't help herself and she smiled back at Tom.

"Are you going to recess?" she asked.

"Yes, I can only walk around, though. I can't run or jump or do cartwheels." Tom laughed and shook his head.

"How are you so happy?" Sofia asked. "You have a grownup with you all the time, it seems. You spilled applesauce on your shirt, and you dropped your fork, you ate your lunch by yourself . . . doesn't that make you grumpy?" she asked.

"Ha! Nope!" Tom said. "If I got upset about everything that went wrong, I would never be happy. It's better to have a good time when things get messed up instead of letting it get to me."

This struck Sofia in an amazing way.

She had never thought to look at her goof-ups as funny or as a good time. She just let it make her grumpy because she felt like she had done something wrong. "That sure is a different way to think!" she said.

"Yep. It's not always easy, but my hands and legs don't work as well as other people's do, so instead of being angry about it, I just know that I'm going to drop things and run into things and have my grownup monitor to help me out. You know, everyone makes mistakes and gets clumsy sometimes anyway. I just may do it a little more than others."

"Wow. That's a great way to think!" Sofia said, suddenly realizing that she didn't have to be in a grumpy mood all the time. She and Tom walked around recess that day. As soon as Sofia saw a friend, she would introduce Tom and apologize for how she ignored them earlier in the morning.

She and Tom and many of her friends walked around the playground together from that day forward, and Sofia always looked at her fumbles, bumbles, and other mishaps differently. She always tried to find the fun in it, and it turned out to be a great way to deal with anything negative. And when she found herself thinking in a grumpy or bad way, she always thought about Tom and his positive outlook on life, and it would make her smile.

~ ~ ~

What do you think, special friend? Do you ever get grumpy over small things? Is there a different way you could look at life? The moral of this story is to keep your chin up because something could always be worse for you, but if you put a little laughter in your day, you'll find that it helps your happiness go a whole new way.

Grace & the Bad Haircut

Do you ever think about how people see you? Do you worry about how you look or what clothes you wear? Well, you don't need to at all. No matter how you look, what style your hair is, how you dress, or what shoes you wear, you are unique and special on the inside just as much as the outside.

~ ~ ~

Grace is a girl with long auburn hair. If you don't know what color "auburn" is, think of the color of a red fall leaf, and you'll have the color of Grace's hair.

Grace loved to do her hair differently each day, and because it was so long, she could do a lot of things with it. One day she braided it. One day she put ribbons on her hair. One day she wore it up in a bun, and on another day she wore it in a ponytail.

Every day she would walk down the hall to her class, someone would tell her, "Grace! I love what you've done with your hair today!" These compliments made her smile. She liked the attention her hair got her, and she liked that she could be so creative with her hairstyles. Before she went to bed, Grace and her mom would look online to see what they could do with her hair for the next day. It was a ritual that made Grace feel happy, and she enjoyed spending time with her mom.

Grace also enjoyed spending time with her brother, his name was Tony and he was her younger brother. They got along well and played together a lot. They enjoyed going outside and riding bikes together and drawing with chalk to play games like hopscotch or four-square. Today, they were outside and were walking back from the park. Grace was making jokes and trying to get her brother to laugh a lot.

Grace's brother was laughing so hard at a joke she said that he didn't see a crack in the sidewalk when they were going inside. When he tripped, he yelped a little. Grace turned around to see him fall forward, right onto his knees.

"Oh no!" Grace said and ran over to see if her brother was okay. He was just getting up off of the ground when Grace saw that his knee was scraped up.

Although it looked a little bloody, it didn't look too bad. But Grace said, "We should get this cleaned up." She helped her brother into the house and down the hall to the bathroom. Then she called for her mom, who came right away.

After they patched her brother up, Grace felt a bit relieved. With a sigh that everything was okay, Grace turned to leave the bathroom and her mom said to her, "Grace. What is in your hair?"

Grace's hands flew up to her head. She didn't know, but as she raked her fingers through it, they became stuck on something. Grace turned around to look into the mirror. "Oh, no!" she said. It looked like a big, chewy wad of bubble gum. "How did that get in there?" She held her hair up to see that, in fact, the gum had stuck to much of her hair. And the more she moved it, the more hair got attached to it.

"Grace, honey," her mom said, taking Grace's hand in her hand. "The more you move it, the worse it is going to become."

"I'm sorry, Grace," her brother said. "I must have spit my gum out when I fell over." He looked very sorry indeed. His lip started to shake, and his chin began to quiver.

Grace looked at her brother and didn't want him to feel bad. She knew it wasn't his fault, and he wouldn't do something like this on purpose. So she said, "Thank you, Tony. But it was an accident." And she gave him a quick hug. "Mom can get it out for me."

Tony left the bathroom, and as much as they tried with ice, peanut butter, cooking oil, and vinegar. They tried everything they could think of to get the gum out of her hair. But nothing worked. After a while, Grace's mom looked at her and said, "I'm sorry, sweetie. I think we are going to have to go to the hairdresser."

"What does that mean?" Grace asked.

"It means that we are going to have to get the gum cut out. But, hair grows continuously, so even though you can cut it off, it will grow back, okay?"

Grace nodded but felt very sad. She loved her long hair and didn't know if

people would know who she was or if they would even like her after she got it cut. "Okay, Mommy," Grace said with a very small voice."

Her mom came over to hug her. "It's going to be okay, I promise. Just think of it as a new style."

"Okay..." Grace said. "But what if no one likes my new hair? What will I do?"

"Grace, you are an amazing girl with so many talents. You are smart, funny, and have a kind heart. Everyone will love your hair, and they will like you just the same as they did yesterday."

That made Grace feel better. Although when they got to the beauty salon, she was a little nervous about getting her hair cut. She climbed up into the chair and said, "It's been a long time since I had shorter hair. I'm a bit nervous."

The hairdresser smiled at Grace and said, "That is normal. We all get a little nervous when we do new things. I'll make sure your hair looks amazing, okay?"

Grace felt a lot better because she had talked about her feelings, and she nodded her head. Although she did close her eyes when the hairdresser put the scissors to her hair and felt the *snip, snip, snip,* as her long, gummed-up hair fell to the ground.

After a few moments, Grace opened her eyes and looked to see that her hair still kind of looked the same. It was just shorter. Now, it touched the top of her shoulders, but Grace kind of liked it. As a smile broke out on her face, her mom came over and said, "Look! I found some hairstyles we could do for shorter hair."

The next morning, Grace and her mom put new barrettes in her hair and pulled back the sides. She took a deep breath as she climbed the bus stairs and tried not to look the bus driver in the eye.

"Hey! You changed your hair!" Grace looked at the bus driver, said. Grace nodded her head nervously. "It looks great! It's a nice change!" he said as he closed the door. Grace felt a wave of relief wash over her. Thankful to have such a nice bus driver who said some-thing kind.

Of course, the bus driver's wasn't the only compliment she got that day. People she didn't know yet also said that her hair looked very good. And by the end of the day, Grace thought it was a nice acci-dent that got her to change her hair and even thought about thanking her brother when she got home.

~ ~ ~

So, what did you think of Grace's story? Do you know that no matter what you look like on the outside, your inside doesn't change? Hopefully, now you will, and if you ever get gum stuck in your hair, know that there is always a way to fix it! Don't be afraid to be different, your differences are what make you special and unique!

Amelia & The Bully

Have you ever seen someone who looks really, really different than you? What do you think about them? Do you know that they are just like you in some ways but different in others? Do you want to make friends with them? Would you like to ask them questions about where they come from, who their parents are, and what they like and dislike? Those are all great ideas! Just because someone looks different than you do, doesn't mean a thing! You never know what someone is like until you talk to them and get to know them as a person.

~ ~ ~

Amelia walked to school, enjoying the weather. She liked the change from Summer to Fall because the leaves turned beautiful colors, and the smell in the air was great. She really enjoyed herself when the seasons changed from one to another.

This day, however, she heard a lot of boys being rowdy and saw that they were huddled in a circle. Being curious and very smart, Amelia decided that their noises were a bit too loud and kind of mean. So she walked over to the crowd and said, "What are you boys doing? It sounds like you are making fun of something."

She had seen this particular group of boys also bothering a squirrel one time, so she didn't want to have it happen again. When their circle opened up, she saw that they were bullying, but it wasn't a squirrel this time. This time it was a small boy.

Amelia shook her head. "I can't believe that you would pick on someone younger than you." The boy in the center was especially small, but his face grew angrier than it already was. "I'm not younger than they are. I'm in the same grade!" He wiped tears off his cheeks and huffed away from Amelia and the group.

Amelia watched him stomp away. If he was in the other boy's grade, he was in her grade too. He was definitely a lot smaller than all of them, but she felt bad for assuming he was in a lower grade and hurting his feelings. Amelia ignored the crowd of boys and quickly followed after the boy.

"Hi!" she said as she caught up to him. "You're new, right? My name is Amelia." She had to walk pretty fast to keep up,

and he was walking really, really quickly. "Wow. You walk fast."

The boy stopped and stared at her, and his face was still angry. "What do you want?" he snapped.

"I'm sorry I thought you were in a younger grade. I couldn't tell with all those boys crowded around you."

The boy looked surprised. "Oh," he said. "I thought you were going to make fun of me."

"Why would I make fun of you?" Amelia asked.

"Because I'm so short."

Amelia shook her head. She knew that being short meant nothing about what a person is like. "Just because you're short doesn't mean you will stay short. Our bodies grow differently, and they change every day. Plus, what you look like on the outside doesn't matter. It's what is inside that counts." Amelia pointed at her heart and her head. "What is your name?" she asked.

The boy blinked at her as if he had never heard anyone say what she had just said.

"My name is Justin. Yes, I just moved here," he said as he blew out a breath. "Thank you for helping me out with those guys. They were pretty mean."

"Sadly, they get like that sometimes. I don't know if they get bored or if they just don't know how to talk to other people."

"Wow. You are nice about them."

"No, it's not okay what they did to you or anyone!" Amelia didn't want to talk about bullies anymore, though. Instead, she wanted to talk about Justin and where he came from. She asked, "So, where did you live before?"

Justin and Amelia talked into the school. They sat at lunch together, and they had a lot of laughs. Amelia found out a lot of really interesting things about Justin. He was short, but his whole family was short. And, he was also fast. Really, really fast. Justin also knew a lot of jokes, some of the jokes Amelia had heard before, but others were jokes that Justin made up on his own. This fact impressed Amelia the most because that meant he made up the jokes, which meant he was really, really funny.

In fact, Amelia and Justin formed such a good friendship that Amelia invited Justin over to her house, and Justin told some of his jokes to her parents and made them laugh too. She was very happy she'd met Justin.

One day, when all the students were at recess, the group of rowdy boys challenged all the other kids to a race. Amelia knew that they were only doing it to make fun of the kids who didn't finish quickly, but Justin wanted to prove to them how fast he was, and so he was the first kid to step up.

The boys laughed at him, and Amelia rolled her eyes. She said to her friend, "Just show them how fast you really are! Then they will see how wrong they are to treat people the way they do." Amelia gave Justin a fist bump, and because of his confidence Amelia was happy to see that other kids stepped up to race with him, beside the group of boys who liked to pick on everyone.

She stood at the front of the race line and said, "Ready? Set. Go!" And the group of students took off running. Justin took off at his super-speed, and Amelia could hear the kids watching the race shout and cheer in amazement at what he was doing.

Justin crossed the finish line first and was barely out of breath. When the other group of bully boys finished, they were huffing and puffing, and it took them a few moments to begin breathing nor-mally again.

Everyone around them cheered. Ame-lia raced over to Justin and hugged him. "That was really fast! You should try out for the track team next year!" Amelia shouted over the cheers.

One of the bullies named Michael came over to Justin and said, "Wow! We are sorry we made fun of you!"

Justin nodded to Michael and looked at Amelia with a smile. "I think that maybe you shouldn't treat anyone or anything differently, because we all have things we are good at."

Michael nodded back at Justin. "You're right! I shouldn't treat people differently. Thank you for racing with me. I had a lot of fun."

Amelia was not surprised at how Justin reacted as they all ran off to race again together. Justin was a very nice boy who had a lot of special talents, and Amelia made a quiet note to always treat people as kindly as Justin did. And she knew that she was going to have to practice running some more if she was to keep up with Justin when running; he was so fast!

~ ~ ~

No matter what size, shape, or color, all people can do something you may never have thought of. Keep in mind, wonderful reader, that your insides make your heart and head who you are. These are the parts of you that count the most. If you are kind, smart, and nice to people no matter what, you'll find people who'll treat you the same way.

Nadia & Her Grandpa

Do you have someone in your life who loves and supports you? Do you go to that person when you need some help? Do they guide you and boost you up when you are feeling down? Like

everyone, we all have bad days and good days. We feel all emotions, whether positive or negative. And sometimes, the person who loves and supports us the most needs our love and support as well. It's important to give as well as get. And when someone we know is having a bad day, it takes a special girl to do something nice for them.

~ ~ ~

Nadia and her grandfather stood beside the table, putting the finishing touches on the model sailboat. They were very quiet, and while Nadia couldn't look at her grandpa because she knew they would start giggling together, even though they were in a serious moment, she knew that his eyebrows were knitted together to look like one big bushy caterpillar.

Grandpa pulled the last bit of string up the mast to finish the sail on their miniature sailboat. She held her breath as he slowly pushed the thread through the tiny hole and tied the whole sail to the top. Once he was done, he turned to look at Nadia and smiled. "Ah, granddaughter, we have finished another one!"

He stood up and picked up Nadia as they did their "finishing dance" together.

"Come now," he said, putting Nadia down. "Let us go eat some cookies and drink some tea."

Nadia didn't really know what part of building toy sailboats she enjoyed most, but she did know that she loved any time she could get when she spent it with her grandpa. After their snack, they went down to the pond in his backyard and fished for a little while. It was a little late in the day to catch anything, but they always enjoyed just being together.

On a normal toy boat building day, Nadia and her grandpa would fish in the morning and then start, but today was a special day. Today they finished the boat, and Nadia was too excited to stand still enough for fishing, so grandpa listened to her stories instead and as he put the final touches on another boat.

They had been doing these same things for years. Fishing, building toy boats and then sailing them on his pond. Her grandpa was a toymaker, and his favorite thing to make was toy boats. Nadia had helped him since she could stand, and before that, her parents told her she would watch him build from her high chair or her play area.

Since before she could remember, they always danced their "finishing the boat dance," and they always had a cookie and tea after each building day. Her grandpa was a very special person to her.

As she got older, they spent a lot less time together because Nadia had started school. Now, Nadia only saw her grandpa on the weekends and special occasions, like her birthday. But even though they saw each other a little less, their special traditions kept happening.

One day, Nadia got a bad grade on an assignment she thought she had done really well on. The grade made her grumpy for the rest of the day, and while the day didn't go particularly bad, even little things frustrated her, for example, she slammed her hand against her desk and she spent her lunch crying, while her classmates made fun of her. Once she got home, she stormed up to her bed-room without even saying anything to her dad, and when he knocked on the door, Nadia couldn't hear him because she was crying so loudly. Soon she had cried herself to sleep and didn't wake up until she heard a soft knock on her door. "Hello, Nadia." She heard Grandpa's voice and instantly sat up. She saw his big smile as he came into her room. "Your dad said that something is wrong and I wanted to come over to see if there was anything I could do."

Nadia didn't know what could make her feel better, so she shrugged her shoulders, but she was happier just knowing he wanted to help her out. Grandpa put his arm around Nadia, and she laid her head on his shoulder. "Do you want to talk about it?" he asked.

She wasn't sure, but once she started talking about her bad day, she couldn't stop. Nadia showed grandpa her sore finger and told him about the kids who made fun of her when she cried at lunch. Even though her voice got a little shaky, she felt stronger by his side and better just because he listened when she told the story again.

"Everyone has bad days and meets people who try to make them feel bad about themselves. It is how you choose to react to the badness and the people that makes you who you are. If you choose to keep feeling bad, you are choosing to stay uncomfortable. If, though, you let go of the bad feeling, you understand that those people who made fun of you are very unhappy too."

Grandpa poked at Nadia's heart. "You are a strong girl. Give the badness away."

Nadia listened to Grandpa and nodded. Although the things that happened to her were bad, she wanted to let go of the bad feeling, so she closed her eyes and decided to feel better. "That's good, Nadia, now replace your bad feelings with good ones. Tell me one good thing about today."

Nadia opened her eyes and smiled. "You came over to help me feel better!"

Grandpa laughed. "Very good! I like that good feeling too! I am happy to see you!'

"Will you eat dinner with us?" Nadia asked.

"Yes! I will stay for dinner."

After dinner and once grandpa had left, Nadia was getting ready for bed. She said to her dad, "Grandpa always helps. I wish I could do something special for him to thank him for everything."

"What do you want to do?"

"I think I want to make him a special toy boat."

"Well, then, you should do it. Do you want my help?"

Nadia knew that her dad would have to help buy the supplies and read some instructions, but otherwise, she wanted to do the boat independently. She knew just the right colors she wanted to use and how she wanted them to be decorated. And so, once her dad bought her the supplies, she started to work on the toy boat every day after school for a little bit.

Since she had helped her grandpa do the boats for so many years, it didn't take her very long to put the model together. But it did take a little while to paint and decorate the boat. At the end of the painting, she named the ship "Grandpa" and added the name to the side. And once the paint dried, Nadia and her dad took the boat over to Grandpa. It was all wrapped up, so he wouldn't know what it was.

When Grandpa opened the door, Nadia yelled, "Surprise! I have a present for you!" And they all went into the house together. Once they sat down at the table, Grandpa opened up the present and saw Nadia's boat.

"Thank you for the lovely boat, Nadia!" He said, laughing, "This boat is the best thing I have ever seen."

Nadia smiled. "Thank you for being a great grandpa! You are always there to help when I need it. I love you so much." She hugged him, and then Nadia, her dad, and Grandpa went out to sail the new toy boat Nadia had made, almost all on her own.

~ ~ ~

Well, I hope you enjoyed the story! Did you know that having people to love and support you can help you out when you don't need it? Do you thank your special grown-up enough? If they don't live in your house, maybe you should call, write, or see them tell them how great you think they are!

Marie the Soccer Star

Have you ever enjoyed something so much you thought you'd want to join a team to do it? Did you get nervous when you went to the first practice? Guess what? That is normal! We all get nervous sometimes, especially when we try something new. But, the great thing is that even when we are scared, we can do the things we love anyway, and that fear and nervousness go away quickly.

~ ~ ~

Marie loved playing soccer but had never joined a team because she was too shy to play around other people. She finally decided to ask her mom to sign her up, because she wanted to play with a team. The wall was not good for kicking the ball back and she also wanted to learn new tricks.

Marie decided that although she was nervous about playing soccer around with a team, that learning new tricks and hanging out with kids her age was going to be worth it once she got to play in a real, live game.

Just thinking about the referees, the goalies, and running on a field got her very excited. For the weeks leading up to the team's first practice, Marie could be found dribbling the ball outside, practicing kicking, even having fun by bouncing the ball off of her knee and, once in a while, her head.

But something began to happen. The closer the first day of practice got, the more nervous she became.

A few days before her first practice, her dad came up to her and asked, "Are you excited about soccer practice?"

Marie stopped what she was doing and looked at her dad. She wasn't. She was scared. "No." Marie said quietly. "I don't think I want to play on a team anymore."

"Oh." Her dad nodded. "Because you are so shy around other people?"

Marie nodded. She got very quiet when other people were around. She liked talking one-on-one with people like her friends Rya and Grace, but when it came to speaking to new people when there were a lot of things going on? She tried to hide in the corner, so that no one paid attention to her.

Her dad took her hand and said, "Listen, Marie. Everything is going to be amazing. You are a fantastic soccer player. Once you get on the field with other kids your own age, your nerves are going to fade away."

Marie took a deep breath and nodded to what her dad said. It did make sense, and her dad was a pretty smart guy, so Marie figured she should listen to him. And for a little while she felt better.

However, when she woke up, she realized that she was still thinking about all the people looking at her while she played soccer. Then she thought about all the teammates on her soccer team.

She worried that maybe she wouldn't be able to play soccer as well as they could because she had never played on a team. Then she worried that she might let them down by not doing something on the soccer field right. Then she got nervous that maybe she would score in the wrong goal! Her stomach started to feel very gurgly. She thought that maybe the idea of being on a soccer team was a big mistake.

When she went down to breakfast the day of her practice, she decided that she wouldn't go. She was too nervous and too scared. She sat down and watched as her dad made breakfast for her and said, "Dad. I'm not going to play soccer today with the team. I decided I don't want to do it." Although it felt awful saying it, Marie felt torn. She didn't want to play around with other people because the idea made her nervous. But, she also did want to play in a real soccer game.

Marie's dad came and sat down next to her. He put his hand on her shoulder and said, "Marie, I know you are nervous about playing in front of people. But let me tell you a little secret, we *all* get nervous before we do anything new. Every. Single. Person. And if you don't get nervous about something, it means that it's not that important to you. Nervousness is normal. But once you go and do the thing you're most afraid of, you're going to feel that fear go away."

As she listened to her dad talk, she realized that he was right! There had been plenty of other times when she had gotten nervous when she was first doing something, and then the butterflies in her belly went away once she tried it.

"Okay, Dad. I'll do it!" she said and hugged her dad. "Thank you for listening to me."

When Marie went to practice that day, she saw a bunch of girls huddled up together. They were all standing around and acting nervous too. Although Marie felt shy, she also remembered what her dad had said about trying something new, so Marie went up to the girls, smiled, and said, "Hi! I'm Marie. What are your names?"

Soon the girls were talking, laughing, and having a good time. When the coaches came up, Marie saw that her dad was in the group. It was a nice surprise. She ran over to hug him and said, "I didn't know that you were going to be a coach."

He laughed and said, "I'm just helping the coaches out. I thought it would help you with any nervousness you had."

Marie was happy her dad was there, even though her nervousness had gone away.

"Come on, team," called the head coach. "Let's get practicing."

After a few practices, Marie found that she was just as good as her other team-mates, and she taught them some new tricks. It was really fun.

The day of the first game came, and so did Marie's nervousness.

Marie was determined to never let her fear stop her again. So she closed her eyes and took a deep breath. She remembered what her dad said about being nervous, that everyone was feeling it, and it helped her feel better.

Marie opened her eyes and looked out at the soccer field. When the whistle blew, she started running to get the ball. When Marie caught up to the ball, she kicked it backward and did a spin to keep up with it. She dribbled and kicked her way through the other team of girls until she got to the goal.

Marie gave the ball a final kick, and it sailed through the air. Even though the other team's goalie got close to blocking it, the ball soared right past her fingers and flew into the goal. Marie jumped up into the air, so excited.

She scored her first goal! She was so happy, and she couldn't wait until she could do it again.

~ ~ ~

Thanks to Marie's dad for reminding us that everyone gets nervous, and it's a sign that whatever we are feeling scared of is important to us! Also, what a great ending! Marie scored her first goal because she let herself let go of her fear and did what she wanted to do. What do you think? Do you think it's normal to have fears and doubts now? Do you realize that even though you are afraid, it doesn't mean that you still can't try something hard and do it with courage? When you do, you are sure to overcome your fears and nerves!

Epilogue

Now that you've read the stories about these wonderful girls and the challenges they overcame, do you know that you can do this too? You are a very special girl, and there is only one of *you* in the world. Whenever you feel scared, nervous, or afraid, make sure to take a deep breath and keep moving forward. That is one of the ways you're going to accomplish many great things in the world.

Remember, the light you have inside of you is the only one of its kind. You are unique, and you are special.

You are an amazing girl.

Bonuses

Our Gifts For You

Subscribe to our Newsletter and receive these free materials

Scan
Me

www.specialartbooks.com/free-materials/

Stay Connected with Us

Instagram: @specialart_coloring
Facebook Group: Special Art - Kids Entertainment
Website: www.specialartbooks.com

Impressum

For questions, feedback, and suggestions:

support@specialartbooks.com

Nadia Ross, Special Art

Copyright © 2022

www.specialartbooks.com

Images by © Shutterstock

Made in the USA
Las Vegas, NV
28 September 2024

509a2e1e-03f5-45e7-b1ec-87c1fd6ef914R01